FLUFFINSTUFFIN

BY MAX ZIEGENHAGEN

Author/ Illustrator- Max Ziegenhagen

Editor- Jennifer Rees

Designer- Sunny Duran

First edition:
ISBN 979-8-9863156-0-7 (hardcover)
ISBN 979-8-986-3156-1-4 (paperback)
ISBN 979-8-9863156-2-1 (ebook)

To Audrey & Declan,
From whom the siblings in this story derive their names and
personalities. May you both be filled with joy and free from fear.

– Love Dad.

In a town not far from you and I,
Lives a group of birds who cannot fly.
What's odd is that they do not try,
But, soon, you'll know the reason why.

The town is called Fluffinstuffin,
Named so by Fat Fluff MacGuffin.
Long, long ago, they gave up flight,
Likely due to fear and fright.

Fluffinstuffin, place of rest,
Where no bird's put to the test.
A town of cozy and of calm,
A town where nothing could go wrong.

Because no bird would ever try
Something crazy as to fly,
Or risk or want or push or strive
Best to eat and sleep and thrive.

For what they did not realize
Was what they did was compromise.
For reasons they had long forgot,
They gave up flight... or so they thought.

Two in town, named Dec and Audy,
Siblings who were seen as naughty,
There with all who never flew
But felt it time for something new.

They hatched and grew up, side by side,
Hand in hand, eyes open wide.
Dec so kind and fun and free,
And Audy brave as one could be.

They often risked, they often tried,
With others watching terrified.
Jumping off of things too high,
Catching things to classify.

One morning Dec, he had a thought,
A thought of what he thought he ought,
To do with wing and tail and feather.
"We should use them all together!"

"What?!" his sister squealed with joy.
This is why she loved this boy!
"You mean to fly?" her question bright.
"Yes, we ought to soon take flight."

They tested wind,
they checked for rain,
Not knowing this was all in vain.
For as they prepped their tiny wings,
They saw some yelling fluffy things.

"Stop! Don't do it, don't you jump,
You'll never fly, you're far too plump!"

The siblings now could see quite clear,
The whole of town seemed to be here.

They were told that they were silly,
Trying to do that which really
Wasn't going to end up well.
Best to stay in bed and swell.

So Dec and Audy stopped and thought,
Thinking thoughts right from that spot,
Confused by things they felt inside,
And feeling still they should've tried.

"There is a stirring in these wings,
As if to use for better things."
Dec and Audy thought and
wondered,
"It's sad that flying's been
surrendered."

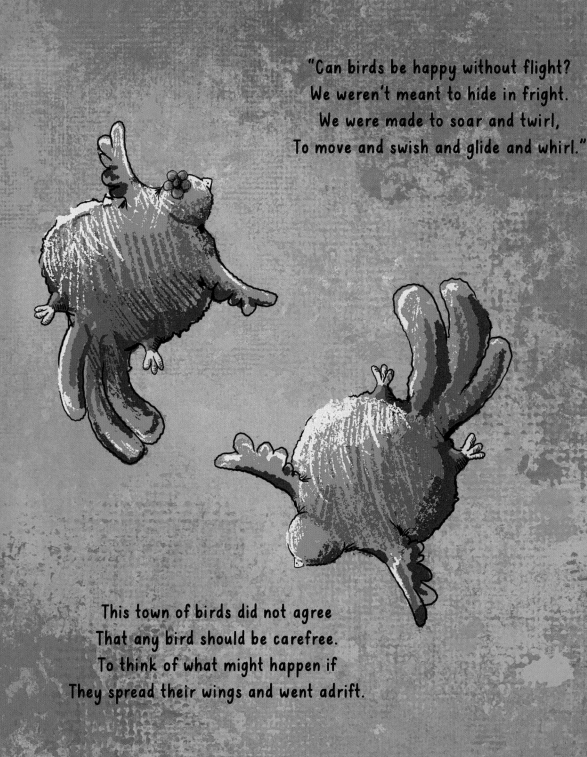

"Can birds be happy without flight?
We weren't meant to hide in fright.
We were made to soar and twirl,
To move and swish and glide and whirl."

This town of birds did not agree
That any bird should be carefree.
To think of what might happen if
They spread their wings and went adrift.

In their hammocks held by ropes,
With little heads all filled with hopes,
That night they dreamed of what could be,
To fly and soar, to live and see.

That morning both popped out of beds,
The dreams still swirling in their heads.
"They can't be right, this cannot be,
We cannot sit here in this tree."

To try at least, to try and fail,
Is better than to sit and wail,
Or rather do nothing at all.
"No way," they chirped, "let's freefall!"

The first attempt they tried and failed.

The second, Dec to no avail

Flapped and flapped and toppled over,

Right into a bed of clovers.

Audy tried to swing from vines,
Thinking she would as it winds,
Round n' round fling up free,

But found herself wound round a tree.

But all their trying ended poorly,
Leaving bumps and feeling sorely.
Feeling they should not have tried.
"We just can't do it!" they both cried.

So those that watched knew they were right,
That birds should never take to flight.
They said so to the siblings here,
With hearts so proud and full of fear.

So off to home, their heads hung low,
shuffling feet and moving slow.
And as they walked in through their door
Both lay down sadly on the floor.

And from his spot their Daddy saw
That his two birdlets felt quite raw.
He set his yummies to one side
And asked if they wished to confide.

Audy stammered, slow to speak,
Words trickling softly from her beak.
"We tried to fly, please don't be mad."
Her words heard gently by her dad.

To hear them try, that made him proud,
But his own fear was speaking loud.
He knew that if they were to soar,
Their perfect safety was no more.

But also thought that he might be
A part of the problem he could see
"Although I cannot fly myself,
I do not want you on the shelf,
Dreaming of what life could be,
Instead of living truly free."

They started hoping more and more,
Maybe they could fly and soar.
"We were meant for more than cozy
More than sleep and eat." And slowly....

Dec and Audy thought and wondered
About their flight attempts and blunders,
As their daddy now had told them,
They were meant for more than boredom.

What if they failed,

What if they fell,

What if they couldn't do it well.

What if they thought they could and couldn't,

What if they wanted to but wouldn't.

"No more what ifs!"

the siblings yelled.

"Let's do it,"

they felt compelled.

On the count of three,
One, two, three... jump!
All eyes on them, all bodies slumped.
With Dad's encouragement still ringing,
They dove and all the while singing.

Down they fell, out of the tree,
Down and down all feathery.
Falling faster, falling hard,
Scared the act would leave them marred.
And just before they bumped the ground...
The two of them popped back around.

And up and over all to see
The soaring little chickadees.
Who moved and swished, glide and twirled,
Around up overhead they whirled.

And Dec and Audy showed that day,
That flying was a better way,

To live, to strive, to risk, to wander.

It's in those things, in the wild blue yonder.

That life is found and lived and breathed,
Not waiting hiding in a tree.

Birds were meant to soar and live...

Dec and Audy certainly did.

Max Ziegenhagen grew up doodling... on everything...
even his homework! As he grew, so did his creativity, and he continues to draw
all the time, be it while watching tv or working. He also used to create elaborate
stories in his head, and recently started writing them down. He now lives with his
wife, kids, and cute little dog in Colorado Springs, where he gets to swim, laugh
with his children, open his home to others, and enjoy the great outdoors!

This will not be his last story, but as his first it holds a special
place in his life, and he is thrilled to share it with you.

As fun as this story is, it's founded on a simple yet, in my opinion, profound reality. In the same way we think it funny to consider an entire community of winged creatures deciding they ought not to live as they are, we do the very same thing. People are wired for connection. We exist relationally and are made to thrive only when we live in vulnerable, authentic, honest relationship. We cannot continue to pretend that we can be "ok" in an isolated and disconnected experience. It's as silly as a bird deciding that it ought not to fly. Be bold, and live as you were intended. Enter the wild blue yonder, where building constancy in friendship, intimacy in marriage, connection in family, and warmth in relationship is the pursuit.

– Max